In The Shadows of Jae

A powerful tale of ambition, redemption, and the price of success

Jae Lavell Productions LLC

Jae Lavell

Copyright Page

The Shadows of Jae
Copyright © [2024] by Jae Lavell
All rights reserved.

Published by [Jae Lavell]
Cover Design by [Ideogram](Canva)

For permissions or inquiries, contact:
[Jae Lavell at: jaelavells.etsy.com]

First Edition: [2024]

Introduction
The Shadows of Jae

In the quiet corners of a bustling city, where the neon lights flicker and shadows stretch long into the night, Jae walks a path no one else can see. A man haunted by his past and driven by a relentless desire for truth, Jae finds himself teetering between two worlds—the one he's always known and the one he's only begun to uncover.

When a mysterious event shatters his carefully controlled existence, Jae is thrust into a labyrinth of secrets, betrayal, and danger. Every clue he uncovers seems to pull him deeper into the shadows, where unseen forces conspire to keep their truths buried. But as Jae pieces together fragments of the puzzle, he begins to realize that the answers he seeks may come at a price he isn't ready to pay.

Who can he trust when even his own reflection feels like a stranger? And what will he do when the shadows he's chasing threaten to consume him entirely?

This is a story of survival and resilience, of the darkness we all carry and the light we fight to find. In the shadows, Jae's journey begins—but the question remains: will he emerge stronger, or will he be lost to the darkness forever?

Step into the shadows. The journey is just beginning.

1.Shadows Of Home

Jae Watkins was a child of the streets, born into a world that barely noticed his existence. His neighborhood was a patchwork of crumbling brick buildings and narrow, dimly lit alleys. It was a place where hope was hard to come by. The people who lived there were families from all corners of the world, trying to make a life in the city. But with that diversity came struggles, tension, and the quest for survival. It was a neighborhood where love wasn't a common language, and every day felt like a battle for something better.

Jae had learned early on that he couldn't rely on anyone but himself. His father had disappeared when he was just a young child, and his mother was so consumed by drugs and guilt that she barely held on. By the time he was twelve, he'd mastered the art of disappearing into the background, blending in with the shadows, but his dreams were bright and blinding. He wanted more than the narrow life that was laid out before him. He wanted to escape. He found comfort in two things: music and books. In the quiet moments after the neighborhood's hustle died down, Jae would sit by the window of his small bedroom and lose himself in the world of stories and melodies.

Music was his escape. He'd found an old, battered guitar in a dumpster when he was ten, its strings rusted and body cracked. But to Jae, it was a lifeline. The first time he strummed, the sound was raw and dissonant, much like his life. Yet, as his fingers learned to dance on the frets, the notes began to form melodies—melodies that spoke of pain, hope, and a longing for something beyond the streetlights and sirens

He'd play the guitar until his fingers ached, weaving the pain of his surroundings into soulful chords. The melodies were a comfort, a reminder that beauty could exist even in the darkest of places. But the neighborhood didn't make dreams easy. As Jae grew older, he was constantly pulled between two worlds—the one he envisioned for himself and the one that threatened to pull him under.
There were close calls, moments when the weight of his environment nearly crushed him: friends lost to the streets, the temptation of easy money through dangerous means, and the endless pressure to give up on something better.

At seventeen, tragedy struck. Jae's heart raced as he sprinted up the apartment stairs where he stayed, two at a time. The door was slightly opened, which wasn't like her. His mother always kept it locked. Always. Mom? he called, pushing it open slowly, his voice already shaking. Then there was Silence. The living room was a mess filled with empty bottles, crushed cigarette packs, and the faint smell of something sour in the air. His gut twisted. He knew this scene. He had seen it too many times, but never like this. He shouted Louder this time, Mom...panic settling in as he moved toward the back of the apartment.

There she was, slumped on the bathroom floor, her back against the tub, head tilted at an unnatural angle. A used syringe lay on the cracked tiles beside her. No, no, no...Jae whispered, dropping to his knees. His hands trembled as he shook her. Mom, wake up. Please. She didn't move. Her skin was pale, lips tinged blue. He grabbed her wrist, searching for a pulse. There was Nothing. The world blurred around him as the weight of what was happening crashed down.

This was it. She was gone. He was alone. He pulled his knees to his chest, staring at her lifeless body, numb and paralyzed by the reality that his childhood had just ended in the space of a heartbeat. Jae stood at her funeral, his heart a storm of anger, sadness, and guilt. The streets whispered their temptations—easy money, fast escape—but Jae had always been a fighter. He vowed not to let the streets claim him the way they had claimed his mother. That same night, he sat under a flickering streetlamp with his guitar. The chords he played were heavy with grief, each note a tribute to his mother's memory. The melody swirled in the air, catching the attention of a few passersby who paused to listen. For the first time, Jae realized that his music didn't just belong to him—it had the power to move others.

Life after his mother's death wasn't easy. He crashed on friends' couches and hustled small gigs in bars that reeked of stale beer and desperation. The guitar became his only constant, his weapon in a world that seemed intent on breaking him. He played on street corners, drawing small crowds who tossed coins and bills into his open guitar case. It wasn't much, but it was honest, and it kept him going. One night, after a particularly grueling day of busking, Jae stared at the ceiling of the run-down shelter where he was staying. He thought about his mother, about the father he never knew, and the streets that had tried to shape him. He promised himself that he would rise above it all. Not just for himself, but for the younger version of him—the scared, hungry boy who had dreamed of something better.

Jae's journey was just beginning, but he knew one thing for sure: he was no longer a child of the streets. He was a man with a purpose, armed with a guitar and a story to tell. And he was ready to fight for his dream, no matter what it took

2. Strumming Through the pain

The small bar was dimly lit, its walls lined with posters of forgotten bands and yellowing setlists. The hum of chatter filled the room, punctuated by the occasional clink of glasses. Jae stood on the makeshift stage, his fingers brushing nervously against the strings of his guitar. The mic crackled as he adjusted it, and he could feel the weight of indifference in the air. He took a deep breath, his heart pounding like a drum in his chest. As he strummed the first chord, the noise in the bar didn't falter. A group in the corner burst into laughter, someone shouted an order at the bartender, and a couple argued in hushed tones near the back. For a moment, Jae thought about stopping. What was the point? But he didn't. He leaned into the music, letting the chords carry the weight of his struggles. His fingers moved instinctively as if they knew the song better than he did. Each note was a thread, weaving a story of heartache, loss, and resilience. His voice cracked slightly as he sang the first verse, raw and unpolished but undeniably honest. The room began to shift.

One by one, heads turned toward the stage. Conversations were hushed as the melody reached them. A man at the bar paused mid-sip, his brow furrowing as if the song had struck a nerve. A woman near the front, who had been scrolling on her phone, set it down and leaned forward. Jae kept his eyes closed, unaware of the attention he was drawing. By the second chorus, the chatter had all but died. The room seemed to breathe with him, the audience caught in the gravity of his performance. He opened his eyes to see a sea of faces turned toward him, their expressions a mix of surprise and admiration. For the first time in what felt like forever, Jae felt seen—not just as a performer, but as a person.

The vulnerability he had poured into the music wasn't met with judgment or pity but with understanding. As he reached the final note, the bar was silent. The kind of silence that held weight, heavy with the collective emotion of the room. Then, a single clap broke through, followed by another and another, until the entire room erupted into applause.

Jae let out a breath he didn't realize he'd been holding, a small smile tugging at the corners of his lips. He nodded at the crowd, a quiet acknowledgment of their response, and stepped off the stage, his guitar slung over his shoulder. As he made his way to the bar, people stopped him—some offering compliments, others sharing their own stories of struggle and perseverance. "Man, that song hit hard," said a man with a weathered face. "I felt that. Me too," Jae said softly, realizing for the first time that his pain wasn't just his own. It was something universal, something that connected him to every person in that room. The bartender slid a drink his way, on the house. Jae raised it in a quiet toast to himself, the room, and the music that had brought them together. That night, for the first time in a long time, Jae didn't feel alone.

3. A Chance Encounter

The crowd in the bar was thinning out, conversations fading as patrons wandered out into the night. Jae stood on the stage, meticulously packing up his guitar. He wiped down the neck of the instrument, the familiar ritual giving him a moment to process the whirlwind of emotions that had filled the room earlier. The applause still echoed faintly in his mind, but he couldn't shake the nagging thought: *Was it just a lucky night?*

As he zipped up the worn case, a voice broke through his thoughts. Hey, that was something else. Jae looked up to see a man standing at the edge of the stage, his hands casually tucked into the pockets of a well-fitted blazer. He had an air of confidence about him, the kind that comes from years of experience, though his easy smile softened it. Thanks, Jae said, his tone cautious but polite.

The man stepped closer, tilting his head as he studied Jae. "Where'd you learn to play like that? Jae shrugged, slinging the guitar strap over his shoulder. "Just picked it up. Been playing for a while now. Self-taught? The man let out a low whistle, clearly impressed. "That's not just playing, my friend. That's storytelling. Every note, every chord—you've got something real there.

Jae blinked, unsure how to respond. Compliments like this didn't come often, and when they did, they usually felt hollow. But something about this man's tone felt different— genuine, almost urgent. The man extended a hand. "Marcus James. Jae hesitated for a moment before shaking it. "Jae. Just Jae. Marcus pulled a sleek business card from the inside pocket of his blazer and held it out. The thick cardstock felt expensive between Jae's fingers. Printed in bold, understated letters was: Marcus James | Talent Manager: *Bringing Stories to Life Through Music and Art*

You've got a story people need to hear," Marcus said, his voice steady and sure. "I've been in this business a long time, and let me tell you, talent like yours? It's rare. But what really stands out is the soul behind it. The kind of soul that connects with people.Jae glanced down at the card, his mind spinning. Was this some kind of scam? Another empty promise? He'd met plenty of smooth talkers before, people who claimed they could open doors but never delivered.

Marcus seemed to sense his hesitation. "Look, I get it. You don't know me from Adam. But I'm not here to sell you a dream. I'm here because I believe in what I just heard, and I think others will too. All I'm asking is for you to think about it. Jae looked up, meeting Marcus's gaze. There was something in his eyes—conviction, yes, but also a kind of understanding, like he knew what it meant to doubt yourself, to carry the weight of your own story.
Why me?" Jae asked, his voice quieter now.

Marcus smiled, but it wasn't the polished smile of a businessman. It was warm, almost fatherly. "Because music like yours doesn't just entertain—it heals. And right now, the world could use a little healing. The weight of those words settled over Jae. He thought about the people in the bar earlier, the way their faces had changed as they listened. He thought about his own struggles, the pain he'd poured into his music.

Finally, he nodded. "I'll think about it. Marcus pulled a pen from his pocket and jotted down something on the back of the card. "My personal number. Call me when you're ready. He turned to leave, then paused. "Oh, and Jae? Marcus smiled again, this time with a spark of mischief. "Don't take too long. The world's waiting. With that, he disappeared into the night, leaving Jae standing there, the business card in his hand and a strange, unfamiliar feeling stirring in his chest.

For the first time in years, it felt like the door to something bigger had cracked open. Jae stood frozen on the stage long after Marcus disappeared into the night.

The business card felt heavier than it should have, as though it carried the weight of a decision he wasn't sure he was ready to make. He traced the embossed letters with his thumb, his mind racing. Why me?

The words kept echoing in his head. He thought about his performance earlier, how it had started as just another night, another chance to pour his pain into the strings and let it bleed out through the music. But then the audience had turned their attention to him, and for the first time in forever, he'd felt connected to something larger than himself. But could that connection be real?
Jae's life up until now had been a series of almosts. Almost landing that big gig, almost making enough to feel stable, almost getting through a day without the past dragging him down. The idea of someone seeing potential in him—real potential—felt foreign. Almost suspicious. He doesn't even know me, Jae thought, his mind tugging at the edges of doubt. What if he's just blowing smoke? What if this is just another promise that leads to nothing? But then he remembered the look in Marcus's eyes. It hadn't been one of empty flattery or feigned enthusiasm. It had been steady, firm, like he really believed in what he was saying.
Jae sighed and slung his guitar case over his shoulder, stepping off the stage. The bar was nearly empty now, just the bartender wiping down glasses and a couple of stragglers finishing their drinks.
As he walked to his car, the night air hit him, cool and sharp. He glanced at the card again under the streetlights, Marcus's handwritten number catching his eye. Personal number, Marcus had said. That meant something, didn't it? He hadn't handed Jae off to some assistant or told him to send an email. It was direct, personal, real.

Still, a small voice in the back of his mind whispered: What if you're not good enough? Jae clenched his fist around the card, anger flaring briefly. At himself, at the world, at the weight of his own insecurities. He thought about his father's words from years ago, the way he'd said, "You're going to change the world with that thing," while pointing to Jae's first guitar. It felt like a lifetime ago. Back then, he'd believed it. Now, he wasn't so sure. He unlocked his car and sat inside, tossing the card onto the passenger seat. The silence of the vehicle wrapped around him, broken only by the faint hum of the streetlights outside. His guitar sat in the backseat, its presence a reminder of everything he'd been through and everything he still carried.

You've got a story people need to hear.

Marcus's words lingered, stubbornly refusing to be ignored. Jae leaned his head back against the seat and closed his eyes. Maybe Marcus was right. Maybe the pain he'd been running from—the loss, the doubt, the loneliness—wasn't something to bury. Maybe it was something to share.

But what if he failed? What if putting himself out there, really out there, only led to more rejection, more heartbreak? He opened his eyes and stared at the card again. It was a small thing, barely bigger than a playing card, but in it, Jae saw two paths. One led to the safety of staying where he was, playing in small bars and pouring his soul into music for audiences that might not always listen. The other was uncertain, full of risks and unknowns, but maybe —just maybe—it was the path he was meant to take.

Jae started the car and drove home, the business card still sitting on the passenger seat. As he pulled into his driveway, he picked it up one more time, turning it over in his hands. He didn't know what tomorrow would bring, but for the first time in a long time, he felt a glimmer of something he hadn't dared to hope for in years. Possibility.

4. The Struggle to Rise

Jae sat on the edge of his bed, Marcus's card balanced between his fingers. He had stared at it for days, the embossed letters taunting him with their promise of opportunity. Finally, after one long night of staring at the ceiling, he grabbed his phone and dialed the number. The phone rang twice before Marcus picked up, his voice crisp but warm. "Jae. I was hoping I'd hear from you."

The conversation was a blur. Marcus wasted no time laying out his vision for Jae's future, speaking with the kind of confidence that made Jae feel like he'd already made it. Within a week, Jae was sitting in Marcus's office, a sleek downtown space filled with gold records and photos of artists who had gone from unknowns to legends.
Here's the deal," Marcus said, sliding a contract across the desk. "I'm not promising it'll be easy. Hell, I'm not even promising it'll be fair. But if you're willing to put in the work, I'll make sure the world hears your story. Jae signed.

The climb started fast. Marcus didn't waste time, getting Jae's tracks recorded and uploaded to streaming platforms within weeks. The songs were raw, intimate, and deeply personal—just as Marcus had wanted. One track in particular, *Strumming Through the Pain,* caught fire. Playlists picked it up, and soon Jae's phone buzzed constantly with notifications.

His face started to appear on local flyers, his name attached to events that were bigger than any he'd ever played before. But as the momentum grew, so did the weight on Jae's shoulders.

One night, after a small but packed gig at a downtown gallery, Jae sat backstage, scrolling through comments on his latest track. Most were positive—words of encouragement, stories from listeners who resonated with his lyrics. But one comment hit him hard: "Sounds like just another sad boy with a guitar. Overrated.
He tossed his phone onto the couch and buried his face in his hands. Why does one bad comment outweigh a hundred good ones? Before he could spiral further, Marcus walked in, clapping him on the shoulder. "Great show out there, Jae. The crowd loved it. Jae forced a smile. Thanks. You've got this, kid," Marcus said, his tone firm. "Don't let anyone tell you otherwise. But it wasn't just the pressures of success that weighed on Jae. Old friends from his neighborhood started showing up. Some were genuinely proud of him, offering congratulations and reminiscing about the old days. But others weren't so kind. Don't forget where you came from," one of them said after a show, his tone carrying an edge that made Jae uneasy.

Another night, a guy he hadn't seen in years showed up uninvited at a gig, pulling him aside afterward. "Man, you're doing big things now," he said, his smile a little too wide. "Don't forget to take care of the people who took care of you back then. It was a reminder Jae didn't need. The memories of his old life—of the people he'd hurt and the people who'd hurt him—were never far from the surface. And now, it felt like those memories were reaching out to drag him back down. Then there she was, Maya.
Jae first saw her while playing at a gallery opening—a last-minute gig Marcus had set up to "expand his audience." The space was filled with abstract paintings and well-dressed patrons sipping wine, but Jae's eyes found her almost immediately.

She was standing near a sculpture, her dark curls falling loosely around her face, a soft smile playing on her lips. She wasn't looking at him, but Jae felt an inexplicable pull as if the music he was playing was somehow for her. When their eyes finally met, it was brief but electric. She held his gaze for a moment, then looked away, her smile deepening. After the set, Jae couldn't stop himself from looking for her. He found her near the same sculpture, talking to an older woman about the art. Hi, he said, feeling oddly nervous. She turned, her expression warm but curious. "Hi.

I'm Jae, he said, awkwardly gesturing toward the stage. I was—uh—playing earlier. I know," she said, her smile widening. "You were good. Really good. Thanks," he said, scratching the back of his neck. "And you are…? Maya," she said, holding out her hand. He took it, noticing how her grip was firm but gentle. "Nice to meet you, Maya. She nodded toward his guitar case. "Your music—it's… raw. Honest. It's not something you hear often. Jae felt his chest tighten at her words, the kind of tightness that came from being understood. Thanks," he said, his voice quieter now. "It's all I know how to do.

That night, as Jae packed up his guitar and headed home, he couldn't stop thinking about Maya. She was different— different from anyone he'd met before. And for the first time in a long time, he felt like maybe, just maybe, he wasn't climbing alone. But as he walked through his door, the glow of the evening dimmed. His phone buzzed with a text from an old friend. We need to talk. The climb was getting steeper, and the weight of the past was pulling harder. Jae sat on the worn couch in his small apartment, guitar still resting against the wall where he had set it down minutes earlier.

The glow of the night—Marcus's praise, the crowd's cheers, and the memory of Maya's smile—still clung to him, but the text on his phone screen threatened to shatter it. We need to talk. Jae sat on the worn couch in his small apartment, guitar still resting against the wall where he had set it down minutes earlier. The glow of the night—Marcus's praise, the crowd's cheers, and the memory of Maya's smile—still clung to him, but the text on his phone screen threatened to shatter it. We need to talk.
It was from a name he hadn't seen in a long time: Tyrell. Jae stared at the message, his thumb hovering over the keyboard. Tyrell had been a close friend once—practically family. They'd grown up together in the same run-down neighborhood, sharing dreams of escaping their circumstances. But those dreams had taken wildly different paths, and the last time they'd spoken, it hadn't ended well.

Before Jae could overthink it, his phone buzzed again. Tyrell was calling. Jae hesitated, his finger hovering over the screen. Finally, he took a deep breath and answered. Tyrell," he said, his voice steady but guarded. Jae," Tyrell replied, his tone cool but familiar. "Been a while, man. Yeah, it has, Jae said, leaning back into the couch. "What's up? There was a pause, long enough to make Jae shift uncomfortably. Look, I've been hearing things," Tyrell said finally. "You're blowing up, huh? Music everywhere, people talking about you. I even heard one of your tracks on a playlist at work. Jae let out a nervous laugh. "Yeah, I guess things are starting to happen."

"That's good, man," Tyrell said, his voice softening. "I'm happy for you. But…"

There it was. The but.

"What's going on, Ty?" Jae asked, his tone sharpening. Tyrell sighed, and Jae could hear the tension through the phone. Look, some folks from back home… they've been asking about you. They're wondering if you've forgotten where you came from. You know how it is."

Jae closed his eyes, his free hand gripping his knee. He knew exactly what Tyrell meant. In their old neighborhood, success wasn't just your own—it belonged to everyone. And people didn't always take kindly to being left behind. I'm not trying to start anything," Tyrell continued. "But some of them? They're not too happy. You might want to keep your head down, at least for a while. Jae exhaled slowly, his thoughts racing. "Why are you telling me this?"

"Because I'm looking out for you," Tyrell said, his voice firm. "You're doing something good, Jae. Don't let them pull you back into the mess you worked so hard to get out of. The words hit Jae harder than he expected. Tyrell's voice wasn't accusatory or bitter—it was protective, almost brotherly. I appreciate it, Jae said finally. But I've got things handled.

Tyrell let out a short laugh. "Do you? Because from where I'm standing, it looks like you're walking into some dangerous territory, man. Jae didn't answer right away. He wasn't sure what to say. Just… be careful," Tyrell said after a long pause. "And if you need anything, you know how to reach me.
Yeah," Jae said quietly. "Thanks, Ty."
When the call ended, Jae sat in silence, the weight of the conversation pressing down on him. The glow from earlier was gone, replaced by an all-too-familiar feeling: the pull of the past.

He glanced at his guitar, its strings catching the light from the lamp. I've come too far to go back, he thought, but the doubt lingered. Jae tossed his phone onto the couch and stood, pacing the room. He couldn't let this derail him—not now. But as much as he wanted to brush it off, he couldn't shake the feeling that Tyrell's warning wasn't just a courtesy. The past wasn't done with him yet.

5. A Growing Bond

The café was warm and inviting, the scent of freshly brewed coffee mingling with the faint aroma of baked goods. Jae had only stopped in for a quick caffeine fix, but as he stood in line, he spotted Maya sitting by the window, her curls catching the soft morning light. She was hunched over a sketchbook, her pencil moving fluidly across the page.

He hesitated for a moment, unsure if she'd even remember him. But something about the ease with which she sat there —completely absorbed in her art—drew him closer. Hey," he said, approaching her table. Maya looked up, startled for a split second before recognition softened her expression into a smile. "Jae, right? From the gallery. Yeah," he said, shifting his guitar case on his shoulder. "Mind if I sit?

Not at all," she said, closing her sketchbook and motioning to the chair across from her. Jae set his case down and sat, suddenly feeling awkward under her gaze. "What are you working on?" he asked, nodding toward the sketchbook. Oh, just some rough ideas," she said, brushing a curl behind her ear. "I like to sketch things that catch my eye—people, moments, things I don't want to forget.

Jae raised an eyebrow. "Did I make it into one of those sketches? Maya laughed, her voice light and melodic. "Maybe," she teased. "You'll have to earn a peek, though. They fell into an easy rhythm of conversation, talking about everything from music and art to their favorite spots in the city. Jae found himself opening up in a way he hadn't expected, sharing stories about his struggles and the people who had shaped him.

You've been through a lot," Maya said, her eyes thoughtful. "But it's all in your music, isn't it? That's why it feels so real. Jae nodded, surprised by how much her words resonated. "I guess I don't know how to do it any other way. As the hours slipped by, Jae realized he didn't want the conversation to end. There was something about Maya—her curiosity, her insight, the way she seemed to see straight through him—that made him want to stay.

Several Encounters Later

Their connection deepened with each meeting. Some days, they'd wander through the city, exploring bookstores, galleries, or quiet parks. Other times, they'd sit in the same café, Maya sketching while Jae strummed his guitar softly, testing new melodies.You should let me design your album cover," Maya said one evening, her voice playful but serious.

You'd do that?" Jae asked, surprised. Of course," she said, tilting her head as if studying him. "Your music deserves something unique—something personal. Jae smiled. "If it's anything like your other work, I'd be lucky to have it. As they spent more time together, Jae began to notice the little things about her—the way she bit her lip when she was concentrating, the way her laughter could fill a room, the way she always seemed to know exactly what to say when he felt lost.

Maya, too, was drawn to Jae's quiet determination and the vulnerability he wore like a badge of honor. She admired how deeply he cared about his music and how he didn't shy away from the pain it came from. A Quiet Moment One evening, they found themselves sitting on the steps of an old building, the city lights flickering around them. Jae had brought his guitar, and as he played softly, Maya leaned her head against his shoulder.

"This," she said, her voice barely above a whisper, "this is the kind of moment I'd sketch. Jae stopped playing, his fingers resting on the strings. "Why? Because it's simple," she said, turning to look at him. "And real. And sometimes, that's all you need. Jae didn't respond, but in that moment, he felt something shift—something he couldn't quite name but knew he didn't want to let go

As the weeks passed, Jae and Maya's relationship grew deeper, their connection strengthening with every conversation, every shared laugh, and every quiet moment that didn't need words.

Jae found himself looking forward to their meetings more than anything else in his life. Maya had become his anchor in a world that often felt chaotic. She grounded him with her calm presence, and her unwavering belief in him made the weight of his struggles feel lighter.

One evening, Maya invited Jae to her favorite spot by the river—a quiet stretch of water surrounded by willow trees, the city skyline glowing softly in the distance. She brought a blanket and a thermos of tea, and they sat under the stars as the cool breeze rustled the leaves around them.

Jae pulled out his guitar and started playing, his fingers moving instinctively over the strings. It wasn't a song he'd written, just a melody that seemed to come from the night itself. Maya listened in silence, her sketchbook resting on her lap. When he finished, she looked at him with a softness in her eyes that made his chest tighten. Your music," she said, "it's like you're telling a story without words."

Jae smiled, his gaze dropping to the guitar. "That's the goal, I guess. To make people feel something. Well, you do," Maya said. "Every time. They sat in silence for a while, the only sound the gentle flow of the river. Can I ask you something?" Maya said suddenly, her voice tentative. Of course," Jae replied, looking at her. What scares you the most?" she asked.

Jae hesitated, caught off guard by the question. He leaned back, staring up at the stars as he thought about his answer. Failing," he said finally. "Not just in music, but in… everything. I've worked so hard to get here, but sometimes it feels like I'm still one step away from losing it all. Maya nodded, her expression thoughtful. "You won't lose it," she said firmly. "Because you won't let yourself. And even if things don't go the way you planned, you'll find another way. You always do.

Her words settled over him like a blanket, warm and reassuring. Jae reached out, his hand brushing against hers. Maya didn't pull away. Late Nights and New Beginnings Their time together became a routine Jae hadn't realized he needed. Late nights spent talking on the phone, their voices low and intimate as they shared pieces of their lives they hadn't shared with anyone else. Afternoon walks through the city, discovering new corners of their world together.

Jae began to notice Maya's sketches taking on a new theme: him. He'd catch glimpses of himself in her work—a profile shot as he played guitar, his hand mid-chord, or the way he looked when he was deep in thought. You're making me look better than I do," he teased one day as he flipped through her sketchbook. Artistic license," Maya said with a smirk. "You inspire me, Jae. That's what artists do—we take what moves us and make something of it."

He couldn't find the words to respond, so he kissed her instead—a kiss that felt like the perfect harmony to the melody of their connection. As Jae's career gained momentum, their relationship faced new challenges. He was busier than ever, with studio sessions, meetings, and performances filling his days. Maya was supportive, but Jae couldn't ignore the guilt that crept in every time he had to cancel a plan or cut their time short.
One night, after a particularly grueling day, Jae showed up at Maya's apartment unannounced. She opened the door, surprised but smiling. Hey," she said, stepping aside to let him in. Hey," he said, pulling her into a hug. He held on longer than usual, breathing in the comforting scent of her lavender shampoo. Tough day?" she asked, pulling back to look at him. Yeah," he admitted. "I just... I needed to see you.

Maya cupped his face in her hands, her touch gentle. "I'm here," she said. "I'll always be here. Jae leaned into her touch, grateful in a way he couldn't put into words. Their bond became a source of strength for both of them. Maya started accompanying Jae to his shows, sketching quietly in the corner as he played. Jae found himself performing better when she was there, her presence a reminder of why he was doing this in the first place.

You're my muse," he told her one night as they lay tangled together on her couch. Maya laughed, but there was a shimmer of emotion in her eyes. "And you're mine. Their connection wasn't without its challenges, but it was real, and it was worth fighting for.

6. The Old Past Resurface

People from his neighborhood, those who had watched him grow up, were envious of his Threats were made. It seemed like the more Jae pushed for a better life, the more the dark side of his past wanted to pull him back down.
One night after He'd just finished a late night session at the studio, Jae found his car keyed, deep scratches carved across the hood. He stood there under the flickering streetlight, hands clenched into fists, staring at the damage. The neighborhood wasn't safe, but this felt different, it felt personal.

The next week, a text came from an unknown number: Don't forget where you came from, Watkins.
The more he climbed, the heavier the shadows grew, threatening to choke the light he was fighting so hard to find. On another night, after a particularly intense performance, Jae returned to his apartment to find a message scrawled on his door,You don't belong here.
The past he thought he had left behind was coming for him, and it was only a matter of time before things would escalate. But this time, Jae wasn't alone.

It was past midnight, and the city outside their window was quiet, the distant hum of traffic barely audible.

Jae sat on the couch, head in his hands, his body tense from a long day in the studio, where the pressure had been relentless.
Maya knelt in front of him, gently pulling his hands away from his face. You don't have to do this alone, she whispered, her voice soft but firm. Jae looked at her, his eyes clouded with frustration and exhaustion. I just... I don't know how to keep going. Every step forward feels like two steps back. Maya sat beside him, her hand resting on his shoulder. Then lean on me, she said, her eyes steady, full of understanding. We'll take those steps together.

They sat in the quiet for a moment, the weight of their struggles hanging in the air between them. But in that silence, there was something else, an unspoken strength they shared, a connection neither of them had ever experienced before. Jae exhaled slowly, letting the tension drain from his body, and rested his head on her shoulder.

Maya wrapped her arms around him, holding him close, their breaths synchronizing, the comfort of her presence became a lifeline he hadn't known he needed. At that moment, they weren't just two people fighting separate battles. They were a team, standing together against whatever storm was waiting on the other side.

With Maya by his side, he faced his problems head-on. Together, they navigated the difficult balance between rising above their past and keeping their integrity intact. It wasn't easy. There were moments of fear and of doubt. But through it all, they stood together, leaning on each other in ways neither of them had ever known before.

Jae's story wasn't just one of survival—it was one of triumph. He had defied the odds, pushed through the darkest moments of his life, and built a future that was entirely his own. And as he stood on the stage at his first sold-out show, with Maya watching from the front row, Jae knew that he had found something even more important than success. He had found the light that would guide him through whatever darkness came next.

As Jae stood on the stage of another sold-out show, the lights blinded him, and the crowd's roar filled his chest with a thrill he'd only dreamed of. I know, Jae said, his voice low, but uncertainty settled in his chest like a heavy stone. He thought leaving the neighborhood, distancing himself from old friends and the dangerous life they led, would be enough.

But they never let go. He had cut ties, but they were still holding the rope, and now it was pulling tighter. Remember who you are, and where you came from. The message was clear: Jae would never truly be free of the streets that raised him. That night, the tension between him and Maya reached its breaking point. She loved him, but the constant fear was wearing her down. I can't live like this, she whispered as they lay in bed, staring up at the ceiling.

Always waiting for something bad to happen. Jae turned to her, his heart heavy. I'll fix it. I'll handle them, Maya. I promise. But the threats escalated. Someone slashed the tires of their car. A brick was thrown through their window with a note tied to it: Remember who you are, and where you came from. The message was clear: Jae would never truly be free of the streets that raised him.

One night, after a particularly tense studio session, Jae returned home to find Maya sitting at the kitchen table, her face pale. She slid a small package toward him. Inside was a photograph—Maya, walking alone downtown, unaware of someone following her. Attached was a note: You aren't the only one we can reach.

Jae's stomach dropped. This wasn't just about him anymore. They were threatening Maya now, and that was a line he couldn't let them cross. I'm done, Maya said, her voice shaky but determined. "I'm not going to live like this. I love you, Jae, but I can't keep pretending we're safe. Not when they're out there, watching us. Jae felt the walls closing in. He couldn't lose her—not like this. But he knew deep down that unless he faced his past head-on, the threats would never stop. The people from his old life weren't going to let him go easily. They wanted to pull him back in, to remind him that no matter how high he climbed, they could bring him crashing down.

A few nights later, Jae went back to the neighborhood—the place he'd avoided for so long. It was time to confront the ones who had been behind the threats, the people who had once been his friends but now saw him as an outsider. When he stepped onto the familiar streets, it felt like stepping into another life. The faces that once welcomed him now watched him with suspicion.
He found them in a dark alley behind a bar, a group of familiar figures who had once been his closest crew.

Their leader, Rico, stepped forward, smirking as he saw Jae. "Back to slum it with us, superstar? Rico's voice dripped with malice. Jae stood tall, his fists clenched.

It ends here. You don't come near me, and you don't touch Maya. We're done. Rico's smile faded, and the tension in the air thickened. Do you think you can just walk away? Forget where you came from? That's not how this works, Jae. Suddenly, one of Rico's guys lunged at Jae. Fists flew, and Jae fought back with everything he had.

It wasn't just about defending himself—it was about protecting his future, the life he had built with Maya, and everything he had worked for. The fight was brutal, but Jae wasn't the same scared kid who had once run from these streets. He held his ground, refusing to let them take him down.
In the aftermath, Jae stood over Rico, blood dripping from his knuckles, breathing hard. Stay away from us, he growled, his voice shaking with both fear and rage. If you ever come near me or Maya again, I swear I'll make sure you regret it.
Rico wiped the blood from his mouth, laughing bitterly. You'll never be free, Jay. You'll always be one of us.
But Jae turned and walked away, leaving them in the alley. As he stepped back into the light of the street, the weight of his past still lingered, but for the first time, he felt something stronger: resolve.
He knew the threats weren't over, but he wasn't going to let them control him anymore.
When he returned home, Maya was waiting for him, worry etched across her face. Jae wrapped his arms around her and whispered, I'm done running, Maya.
It's over. Whatever comes next, we face it together. And together, they braced for whatever the future held, knowing that the shadows might still linger—but the light they'd found in each other was brighter than any darkness.

After that night, Jae and Maya knew things wouldn't change overnight, but they had turned a corner. The threats began to fade into the background, and for the first time in a long while, they could breathe without the constant fear hanging over them.

With the weight of his past slowly lifting, Jae's career truly began to take off. His debut album, a raw mix of soulful melodies and gripping lyrics, hit the airwaves and resonated with listeners. His songs, rich with stories of struggle and redemption, climbed the charts.

The success brought a new kind of freedom—one where he and Maya could finally enjoy the lives they were building. They moved into a loft in the heart of the city, far from the streets that had once held Jae back. Their space was filled with Maya's vibrant paintings and the soft strumming of Jae's guitar as he worked on new music.
It was their sanctuary, a place where they could create, dream, and love without the shadows of the past looming over them.

One evening, after a particularly grueling studio session, Jae surprised Maya with a trip to the coast. The two of them hadn't taken a real break in years, and he wanted to give her a chance to breathe—to thank her for standing by him when things were darkest.
They spent their days walking along the beach, talking about their future, and dreaming of what they could build together. For the first time, Jae felt truly at peace.

Chapter 7: A growing Bond

As the weeks passed, Jae and Maya's relationship grew deeper, their connection strengthening with every conversation, every shared laugh, and every quiet moment that didn't need words.

Jae found himself looking forward to their meetings more than anything else in his life. Maya had become his anchor in a world that often felt chaotic. She grounded him with her calm presence, and her unwavering belief in him made the weight of his struggles feel lighter. One evening, Maya invited Jae to her favorite spot by the river—a quiet stretch of water surrounded by willow trees, the city skyline glowing softly in the distance. She brought a blanket and a thermos of tea, and they sat under the stars as the cool breeze rustled the leaves around them.

Jae pulled out his guitar and started playing, his fingers moving instinctively over the strings. It wasn't a song he'd written, just a melody that seemed to come from the night itself. Maya listened in silence, her sketchbook resting on her lap. When he finished, she looked at him with a softness in her eyes that made his chest tighten. Your music," she said, "it's like you're telling a story without words. Jae smiled, his gaze dropping to the guitar.

That's the goal, I guess. To make people feel something. Well, you do," Maya said. "Every time. They sat in silence for a while, the only sound the gentle flow of the river. Can I ask you something?" Maya said suddenly, her voice tentative. Of course," Jae replied, looking at her. What scares you the most?" she asked.

Jae hesitated, caught off guard by the question. He leaned back, staring up at the stars as he thought about his answer. Failing," he said finally. "Not just in music, but in... everything. I've worked so hard to get here, but sometimes it feels like I'm still one step away from losing it all. Maya nodded, her expression thoughtful. "You won't lose it," she said firmly. "Because you won't let yourself. And even if things don't go the way you planned, you'll find another way. You always do. Her words settled over him like a blanket, warm and reassuring. Jae reached out, his hand brushing against hers. Maya didn't pull away.

Late Nights and New Beginnings Their time together became a routine Jae hadn't realized he needed. Late nights spent talking on the phone, their voices low and intimate as they shared pieces of their lives they hadn't shared with anyone else.

Afternoon walks through the city, discovering new corners of their world together. Jae began to notice Maya's sketches taking on a new theme: him. He'd catch glimpses of himself in her work—a profile shot as he played guitar, his hand mid-chord, or the way he looked when he was deep in thought.

You're making me look better than I do," he teased one day as he flipped through her sketchbook. Artistic license," Maya said with a smirk. "You inspire me, Jae. That's what artists do—we take what moves us and make something of it. He couldn't find the words to respond, so he kissed her instead—a kiss that felt like the perfect harmony to the melody of their connection.

As Jae's career gained momentum, their relationship faced new challenges. He was busier than ever, with studio sessions, meetings, and performances filling his days. Maya was supportive, but Jae couldn't ignore the guilt that crept in every time he had to cancel a plan or cut their time short.

One night, after a particularly grueling day, Jae showed up at Maya's apartment unannounced. She opened the door, surprised but smiling. Hey," she said, stepping aside to let him in. Hey," he said, pulling her into a hug. He held on longer than usual, breathing in the comforting scent of her lavender shampoo. Tough day?" she asked, pulling back to look at him. Yeah," he admitted. "I just... I needed to see you. Maya cupped his face in her hands, her touch gentle. I'm here," she said. "I'll always be here. Jae leaned into her touch, grateful in a way he couldn't put into words. Their bond became a source of strength for both of them. Maya started accompanying Jae to his shows, sketching quietly in the corner as he played. Jae found himself performing better when she was there, her presence a reminder of why he was doing this in the first place.

You're my muse," he told her one night as they lay tangled together on her couch. Maya laughed, but there was a shimmer of emotion in her eyes. "And you're mine. Their connection wasn't without its challenges, but it was real, and it was worth fighting for. The soft glow of the evening sun spilled over the park, casting long, golden shadows. Jae stood near a small wooden bridge over a quiet stream, nervously adjusting the cuffs of his shirt. His guitar rested against a nearby bench, ready to play its part in his plan.

Maya was late—not unusual for her—but Jae's heart pounded all the same. In his pocket was a small velvet box that felt heavier than it should. The past few weeks had been a whirlwind of planning and secrecy, but it all came down to this moment. When Maya finally arrived, her eyes sparkled in the fading light. "Sorry, traffic," she said, leaning in for a quick kiss. No problem, Jae replied, his voice a little shaky. "I was just… enjoying the view. He motioned for her to sit on the bench and picked up his guitar. Maya raised an eyebrow, curious but smiling. I wrote something for you," he said, strumming the first chords.

The melody was soft, sweet, and achingly personal. As he sang, the lyrics spoke of their journey—how she had been his light in the darkest times, how her belief in him had carried him further than he thought possible. Maya's smile faltered as tears welled up in her eyes. When the last note faded, Jae set the guitar aside, dropped to one knee, and pulled the box from his pocket.

Maya, you've been my muse, my strength, and my heart. I can't imagine a life without you. Will you marry me?

For a moment, Maya was speechless, her hands covering her mouth. Then she nodded vigorously, tears spilling over her cheeks. "Yes! Of course, yes! The world seemed to fall away as Jae slid the ring onto her finger and they embraced, the sound of the stream and the rustle of leaves their only witnesses. As the excitement of the proposal settled, the chaos of wedding planning began. Maya's small apartment transformed into command central, with color swatches, fabric samples, and bridal magazines scattered across every surface. Maya's best friends, Serena and Lila, dove in with enthusiasm. Serena, ever the perfectionist, took charge of the planning timeline, while Lila brought her artistic flair to designing invitations and decorations.

Okay, Serena said one evening, her tablet in hand. "We've narrowed the venue down to three options. Rustic barn, modern gallery, or beachside pavilion? Rustic barn," Maya said without hesitation. "It feels… us. Lila nodded. "Great choice. I've got some centerpiece ideas that will blow your mind. Meanwhile, Jae found himself swept into the process in unexpected ways. Maya insisted he help choose the music for the reception. Babe, it's not just a playlist," she said, waving off his protest. "It's the soundtrack to our love story.

The most anticipated part of the preparation came when Maya and her friends went dress shopping. Serena and Lila were buzzing with excitement as they walked into the boutique, ready to play their roles as unofficial fashion consultants. The first dress Maya tried on was beautiful but didn't feel quite right. Neither did the second. Or the third. Then she stepped out in the one. The room went silent. Oh my god, Lila whispered, tears forming in her eyes. "Maya, that's it. Maya turned to the mirror, her breath catching. The dress was simple yet elegant, with delicate lace detailing and a flowing skirt that felt like it belonged to her. For the first time, she could picture herself walking down the aisle to Jae. Late one night, as the wedding approached, Maya and Jae sat on the floor of their apartment, surrounded by seating charts and RSVP cards.

This is a lot, Jae said, leaning back against the couch. Tell me about it, Maya replied, rubbing her temples. But it's worth it," Jae added, his voice soft. Maya looked at him and smiled. "Yeah. It really is. They sat in silence for a moment, their fingers entwined. The wedding would be hectic, and life would continue to throw challenges their way, but in that quiet moment, they felt ready to face it all together.

The morning of Jae and Maya's wedding dawned with a golden hue, as if the world itself was blessing their union. The rustic barn was nestled in a meadow surrounded by wildflowers, their vibrant colors painting the landscape. Maya had insisted on an outdoor ceremony, and nature seemed to agree with her choice.

Maya woke up to the sound of laughter and the scent of fresh coffee. Her bridesmaids, Serena and Lila, were already bustling around the bridal suite. Okay, Maya, today's the day!" Lila chirped, handing her a steaming mug. Maya sat in her silk robe, her heart racing. "I can't believe it's here. Serena rolled her eyes playfully. "You better believe it. Now sit still while the glam squad works their magic. As the hair and makeup artists transformed her, Maya's mind drifted to Jae. She pictured his nervous smile and the way his eyes lit up when he looked at her.

Thinking about him, aren't you? Lila teased, catching her dreamy expression. Maya grinned. "Always. Across the barn, Jae was pacing in his room, tugging at his tie. His best man, Marcus, leaned against the doorframe, watching with amusement. Relax, man. You're not about to go on stage. Well... kind of," Marcus said with a smirk. Jae laughed nervously. This is way bigger than any stage. What if I mess up? What if I forget my vows? Marcus clapped a hand on his shoulder. "You won't. You love her. That's all that matters. Taking a deep breath, Jae nodded. "You're right. She's all that matters.

The guests gathered under a large oak tree adorned with fairy lights and delicate garlands of baby's breath. A gentle breeze rustled through the leaves as soft acoustic music played in the background—handpicked by Jae, of course.

When the bridal procession began, all heads turned toward Maya. She appeared at the end of the aisle, radiant in her lace gown. The sun seemed to catch every detail, making her look almost otherworldly. Jae's breath caught in his throat. For a moment, everything else faded away. It was just her. As Maya walked closer, her eyes locked on Jae's, her smile trembled with emotion. When she reached him, he whispered, "You're breathtaking. And you're mine," she replied softly.

The officiant led them through the ceremony, but the vows stole the show. Jae's voice cracked as he said, "Maya, you've been my strength, my light, and my reason. Today, I promise to always fight for us, no matter what. Maya wiped a tear and said, "Jae, you showed me that love can be a melody we create together. I promise to keep singing with you, even through the storms."

The barn was transformed into a glowing reception hall, with long wooden tables, twinkling string lights, and wildflower centerpieces. The couple's first dance was to a song Jae had written—a surprise for Maya. As he sang the opening lyrics, Maya's hands flew to her mouth. The room went silent, save for Jae's voice and the soft strumming of his guitar. When the song ended, Maya kissed him deeply, and the guests erupted into cheers and applause.

As the night wound down, guests gathered outside with red roses in hand. Jae and Maya emerged hand-in-hand, their faces glowing with happiness. Ready for forever?" Jae asked, looking at her.

With you? Always," Maya replied, her eyes sparkling as brightly as the lights around them.They ran through the tunnel of sparklers, laughter echoing in the cool night air. When they reached their car—a vintage convertible decked out with cans and a "Just Married" sign—Jae helped Maya inside. As they drove off into the night, the barn lights faded behind them, but their journey together was just beginning.

Chapter 8. Shadows in the Dark

The evening was calm, the city humming with its usual rhythm as Jae drove back home an after a late recording session. His guitar case felt heavier than usual, and the streetlights above flickered ominously. He adjusted the strap on his shoulder, his mind buzzing with melodies from the session, but something felt off. It wasn't the music or the late hour—it was the sense of being watched.
Jae glanced over his shoulder. The sidewalk behind him was empty, save for a stray cat slinking into an alley. He shook his head, brushing off the feeling. You're just tired, man, he told himself. But as he turned a corner, he saw a shadow move in the alley ahead. Picking up his pace, Jae kept his eyes forward, but his ears were tuned to every sound— every footstep, every shuffle. Then he heard it: the faint echo of footsteps, matching his stride.
He stopped abruptly, and the footsteps stopped too. Yo, who's there?" Jae called, his voice steady but his pulse racing. Silence. He waited for a moment, scanning the dimly lit street. Then, out of nowhere, a figure stepped into the light—a tall man in a dark hoodie, his face obscured by the shadows. Can I help you?" Jae asked, his voice firmer now. The man didn't answer. Instead, he took a step closer.

Jae's instincts kicked in. He tightened his grip on the guitar case and turned to walk away, but the man's voice stopped him. You think you can just leave the past behind, Jae? Jae froze. The voice was unfamiliar, but the words hit him like a punch to the gut. What do you want?" he asked, turning back around. The man chuckled darkly. You've got a lot of people asking that question lately. Guess you'll find out soon enough.

Before Jae could respond, the man turned and disappeared into the alley. Jae hesitated, torn between chasing him and walking away. He decided to follow, his heart pounding as he stepped into the darkness. The alley was narrow and lined with dumpsters. Jae could hear the man's footsteps echoing, but as he turned another corner, he found himself alone. Hello? he called out. No response. Just as he was about to leave, Jae noticed something on the ground—a crumpled piece of paper. He picked it up, his hands trembling as he unfolded it.

Scrawled in jagged handwriting were the words: The past never stays buried. Watch your back. Jae's mind raced as he stood there, gripping the note. The shadows around him seemed to close in, and he felt the weight of the moment settle heavily on his chest. Who was this man? And what did he know about Jae's past? For the first time in years, Jae felt the chill of his old life creeping back into his new one. The night felt heavier as Jae stared at the note. His hands trembled, not from fear but from the weight of the past he'd buried—the people he had hurt, the bridges he had burned, and the dangers he thought he'd left behind.

But the shadows were catching up, and they weren't going to wait for him to decide what to do next.

The next morning, Jae sat on the edge of his bed, the note and photograph still on the table. He knew he couldn't ignore this, but the question was how to respond. He didn't want Maya or Marcus to know—he couldn't risk dragging them into this mess.

Instead, he called someone who might have answers. Jules, Jae said as soon as the call connected. Jules had been a close friend in the old neighborhood, someone who always had their ear to the ground.

Jae? Jules sounded surprised. "Man, I thought you fell off the map. Not exactly, Jae said. "Listen, I need to know if Rico's been stirring things up. He came to see me last night, left a note. Jules went quiet. "Rico's been talking. He's been bragging about how you 'owe' him. He's trying to make it sound like you ran off with something that belongs to him. That's not true, Jae said, anger flaring in his chest. Doesn't matter if it's true. Rico's all about appearances, and now that you're getting some buzz, he's thinking you're his payday. Watch your back, Jae. Rico's not the only one watching you.

Later that day, Jae found himself back at the studio, but his mind wasn't on music. As he strummed his guitar, his hands moved on autopilot, the haunting words from the note echoing in his head. The door to the studio creaked open, and Jae looked up to see Marcus stepping in. You good, man? Marcus asked, setting his briefcase down. Yeah, Jae lied, though his expression said otherwise.

Marcus frowned but didn't push. Instead, he handed Jae a flyer for an upcoming showcase—a high-profile event that could launch Jae's career to a new level. This is your chance," Marcus said, smiling

Big stage, big audience. You ready? Jae nodded, but inside, he wondered: Can I handle this when my past is hunting me down? That night, as Jae walked to his car, he spotted someone leaning against it—Rico. You didn't think you could call Jules and I wouldn't hear about it, did you?" Rico said, a twisted grin on his face. Jae clenched his fists, his voice steady but laced with anger. What do you want, Rico? Money? Revenge? Spit it out."

Rico stepped closer, his tone venomous. "You were supposed to be one of us, Jae. You don't get to leave and act like we never existed. So here's the deal: you've got something people want—your music, your story. You're gonna share some of that success. Or I'll make sure no one hears your songs again. The threat was clear.

A few days later, Jae was in the middle of a tense phone call with Jules when Maya walked into the room. He didn't notice her at first, his voice low and sharp. I don't care what Rico's saying," Jae hissed into the phone. I'm not playing his game. I'm done with that life. Jae?" Maya's voice cut through his focus like a knife. He spun around, his heart sinking. Maya stood there, her arms crossed, her expression a mix of confusion and hurt.

Who's Rico? she asked. Jae sighed, running a hand through his hair. "It's… complicated. Well, uncomplicate it," Maya said, her tone firm. "You've been distant, jumpy, and now you're on the phone talking about 'that life'? What's going on? Jae sat down heavily on the couch, his head in his hands. After a moment, he began to speak, his voice quiet but steady. Before all this—before the music, before us—I wasn't the guy you know now," he said. "I ran with people I shouldn't have. Did things I'm not proud of. Rico was part of that world. Maya sat beside him, listening intently.

I thought I left it all behind," Jae continued. "But Rico's back, and he wants to pull me into his mess again. He thinks I owe him something because I walked away. Maya was silent for a long moment. Then she reached out, taking his hand in hers. Why didn't you tell me?" she asked softly. Because I didn't want to drag you into it," Jae said. "I wanted to protect you. Maya shook her head. "Jae, we're in this together. Whatever it is, we'll face it. But you can't shut me out. That's not how this works.

With Maya's support, Jae felt a new sense of resolve. They agreed that ignoring Rico wouldn't make him go away. Instead, Jae needed to confront his past head-on—but on his terms. That night, as Jae sat with his guitar, Maya came up behind him, wrapping her arms around his shoulders. You're not alone in this, she said. Whatever happens, we'll handle it. For the first time in days, Jae felt a flicker of hope. He strummed a chord, the sound ringing out strong and clear.

Chapter 9: Shadows Closing In

The tension reached a boiling point a week later when Rico decided to escalate his threats. It started with a cryptic voicemail. Nice set you played last night," Rico's voice drawled. Be a shame if something happened to your shiny new reputation. Jae deleted the message, but the unease it left lingered. That same day, a package arrived at the studio. Inside was a single black glove and a note: *Don't make me come find you.* Jae paced the living room, the package still on the coffee table. Maya watched him, her jaw set in determination. This has to stop, she said. He's not going to back off until you face him. And say what, Maya? Please stop threatening me'? Rico doesn't work like that.

Maya crossed her arms, her expression fierce. Then we don't ask. We fight back. Jae blinked. Fight back? You're serious? Yes, Maya said. We're not running, Jae. He's trying to intimidate you because he thinks you're scared. But what if we make him the one who's scared? Over the next two days, Jae and Maya worked together, brainstorming a way to confront Rico without putting themselves in immediate danger. Maya reached out to a friend from her PR circle who specialized in crisis management. Meanwhile, Jae got in touch with Jules, hoping his old friend could provide some leverage. I can't just roll up on him, Jae said to Jules over the phone. I need to hit him where it hurts. Rico's got two weaknesses, Jules said. Money and his ego. If you can mess with either of those, you've got a shot. Maya chimed in from across the room. "What about exposing him? If he's tied to illegal stuff, we could make that public. Smart, Jules said. "But be careful. Rico's got ears everywhere. If he thinks you're planning something, he'll come at you harder. With Jules' help, Jae and Maya devised a plan. Jules would leak a rumor that Jae was willing to pay Rico off—but only if Rico showed up in person to discuss terms. Meanwhile, Maya worked with her PR friend to ensure that the meeting would be discreetly monitored. They needed evidence of Rico's threats to use against him if things escalated further. I don't like you being there, Jae told Maya as they finalized the details. And I don't like the idea of you doing this alone, Maya shot back. "We're in this together, remember? The meeting was set at a dimly lit bar in a quiet part of town. Jae sat in a booth, his guitar case leaning against the wall beside him. The air was thick with tension as Rico strolled in, his usual smirk firmly in place. Well, well, Rico said, sliding into the booth across from Jae. I didn't think you had it in you to call me. Jae leaned forward, his voice steady.

This ends here, Rico. I'm not paying you a dime, and I'm not letting you ruin what I've built. Rico chuckled, his grin widening.
You think you can just say no to me? You owe me, Jae. Everything you've got, I made possible. Behind them, Maya sat at the bar, keeping a careful eye on the exchange. She discreetly texted their PR contact, signaling that the conversation was heating up. You didn't make me, Jae said, his voice rising. I walked away from you, and I've earned every bit of success I've got now. You don't own me.

Rico's smirk faltered, replaced by a flash of anger. You've got guts, I'll give you that. But guts won't save you when things start falling apart. Before Rico could say more, Jules walked in, flanked by two men Jae recognized from the old neighborhood. They didn't look happy. Rico, Jules said, his tone cold. We need to talk. Rico froze, his bravado slipping. What's this about?
Jules crossed his arms. You've been running your mouth, making threats, and dragging us into your mess. That's over. You want to go after Jae? You'll have to deal with us first. For the first time, Rico looked unsure. He glanced around the bar, realizing too late that he was outnumbered and outmaneuvered.

With Rico's power play effectively neutralized, Jae and Maya finally breathed a sigh of relief. They had the recordings of Rico's threats, thanks to Maya's planning, and Jules made it clear that the neighborhood wouldn't tolerate Rico's antics anymore. As they left the bar, Jae took Maya's hand, his gratitude evident in his eyes. You were amazing, he said. So were you, Maya replied, squeezing his hand. We make a pretty good team

10. Family Betrayals

Jae was at the top of his game. His album had just gone platinum, and every door that had once been locked to him was now wide open. But with success came new problems. The weight of his old life still pressed against his back, no matter how far he tried to run from it. The threats had slowed, but Jae knew better than to relax completely. He still hadn't shaken the feeling that someone was watching, waiting for him to slip up.

Maya had gone out for the evening, leaving Jae to sit on the balcony of their loft, his phone buzzing with texts and emails from agents and producers. He leaned back, taking a breath, grateful for the silence. But then his phone buzzed again—this time with a message that sent a chill down his spine.

You think you're safe, but we know everything. You're never out of reach. Jae's heart pounded in his chest as he stared at the screen. He had received these kinds of messages before, but this one felt different. There was something unnervingly specific about it as if they knew more about him than they should. He texted his manager and told him he wasn't feeling well, canceling all of his meetings for the next day. He needed time to think, to figure out what was happening.

But the more he thought about it, the more it nagged at him. Someone was feeding his old enemies information— someone close. The following night, Jae got a call from Rico, his old crew leader. His number was blocked, but Jae knew who it was the moment he heard the voice on the other end. We need to talk, Rico said, his voice low and laced with menace. Face to face.

Jae's stomach churned. I'm not interested. We don't have anything to talk about. I think you'll want to hear what I have to say. It's about your family.

Jae froze. Family? How could they have any leverage over him now? His ties to the old neighborhood were almost completely severed, his only family being his younger brother, Darius, who had supported him from the beginning. Jae had done everything he could to keep Darius away from the mess he had left behind. Rico, Jae warned, if you come after my brother, I swear to—
Your brother? Rico interrupted with a laugh. We don't need to come after him. He's already one of us.
The words hit Jae like a punch to the gut. He gripped the phone tighter. What the hell are you talking about?

Darius has been feeding us information for months, Jae, Rico said smugly. How do you think we've been keeping tabs on you? You think I didn't know about your little retreat upstate or your meetings with the label? All that money, all that success—you think Darius didn't want a cut? Jae couldn't believe what he was hearing. Darius, his own brother? The one person he had trusted unconditionally? He had fought so hard to protect him from this life, and now... this? He's been working with us from the start, Rico continued. It's just business, Jae. He saw an opportunity. Can't blame him for wanting to get a taste of what you've got.

Jae felt like the floor had been ripped out from under him. His mind raced. Had Darius been lying to him this whole time? All the late-night calls, the check-ins, the times he had asked for help—was it all part of a setup?

I don't believe you, Jae finally spat, his voice shaking with both anger and disbelief. Darius would never do that to me. Then ask him yourself, Rico taunted. He's been enjoying the cash flow for a while now. If you don't believe me, take a look at his bank account. It's all there. Jae ended the call abruptly, his heart pounding. Without thinking, he dialed Darius, his hands shaking as he waited for his brother to pick up. After a few rings, Darius' familiar voice came on the line. Yo, Jae, what's up?

Jae struggled to keep his voice calm. We need to talk. Now. I'm coming over. Jae arrived at Darius' apartment in the early hours of the morning, his mind racing with a mix of betrayal and disbelief. He knocked on the door hard, and when Darius answered, Jae could see the guilt flash in his brother's eyes for just a second before he covered it up with a smile. Jae, what's going on? It's late, Darius said, trying to sound casual. Jae shoved past him into the apartment, his fists clenched. Cut the act, Darius. I just got a call from Rico.Darius froze, his face going pale. Rico? What does that have to do with—Don't lie to me! Jae's voice boomed, anger seeping into every word. He told me everything. How long have you been selling me out? Huh? How long have you been feeding them information? All while I've been busting my butt trying to keep you safe. Darius backed up, his hands up in defense. Jae, it's not like that. I didn't have a choice—You always had a choice, Jae snapped, stepping closer. I gave you a way out. I gave you everything. All I ever wanted was for you to stay out of that life, and this is how you repay me? Darius' eyes filled with a mix of shame and anger. What do you expect, Jae? You leave the neighborhood, get famous, and forget about the rest of us? You live in your fancy loft with your perfect life, and I'm supposed to just sit here, struggling, watching you live the dream?

Jae shook his head, his voice low and full of hurt. I was trying to help you, Darius. Everything I did was for you. I left because I wanted you to have a better life, not to drag you down with me. Darius looked away, the guilt finally breaking through. I didn't mean for it to go this far. They… they promised me things, Jae. Money, protection. I thought I could handle it, but it got out of control.

Jae stood there, staring at his brother, the weight of the betrayal sinking in. He had fought so hard to protect Darius from the very thing that had swallowed him up, and now his own brother had become part of the machine that wanted to destroy him. I can't believe this, Jae whispered, his voice breaking. You were supposed to be the one person I could trust. Darius hung his head, tears welling in his eyes. I'm sorry, Jae. I'm so sorry, Jae couldn't hear it. The damage was done. Without another word, he turned and walked out of the apartment, leaving Darius standing alone, the silence between them heavier than it had ever been. The day after the confrontation, Jae woke with a heaviness in his chest that he couldn't shake. He hadn't spoken to Darius since storming out of his apartment. .

The betrayal still stung too much, the wound too fresh. Jae had spent the night pacing, thinking about everything he and his brother had been through—the childhood they had survived, the streets they had fought to escape, and how, somehow, they had ended up on opposite sides. He knew he had been hard on Darius, but the anger had clouded everything. All Jae wanted was to protect him, to keep him safe from the life that had nearly swallowed him whole. But now, Darius was caught in its grip, and Jae felt powerless.

His phone rang, shattering the silence of the morning. Jae glanced at the screen—it was an unknown number. His stomach dropped as he answered. Jae, the voice on the other end said, shaky and unfamiliar. This is Officer Henderson with the 45th precinct. We need you to come down to the station. It's about your brother. Jae's heart stopped. What happened? There was a pause before the officer spoke again, his voice measured. I'm sorry to inform you, but Darius was involved in an altercation last night. He didn't make it. The phone slipped from Jae's hand, crashing onto the floor, but the words kept echoing in his mind. He didn't make it. Jae stood frozen, his world spinning out of control. Darius was gone. His brother—the one person he had spent his life trying to protect, trying to save—was dead.

Jae stood at the edge of the cemetery, the autumn wind cold against his face. The funeral had been small, just a handful of people. His mother had passed years ago, and now Darius was gone too. He watched as they lowered the casket into the ground, his mind replaying every moment they had shared. The fights, the laughter, the plans they had made to escape their old life.

And that last conversation—full of anger, hurt, and betrayal. The memory of it tore at Jae's heart. He wished he could take it back, wished he had told Darius that he forgave him. But it was too late.

Jae knelt down beside the grave, his eyes burning with unshed tears. I'm sorry, he whispered. I should have been there for you. I should have done more. There was no response, just the quiet rustling of leaves in the wind. The guilt weighed heavy on him, but he knew there was nothing he could do now. The streets had taken Darius, like they had taken so many others. And no amount of success or fame could bring him back.

But as Jay stood to leave, he made a silent promise to his brother. He would keep fighting, not just for himself, but for Darius too. He wouldn't let his brother's death be in vain. Jay would carry his memory with him, through every note he played, through every song he wrote.
And maybe, just maybe, that would be enough to keep the shadows at bay.

11. Sabotage in the Spotlight

A few weeks later with the lights dimmed, and the crowd at the packed venue buzzing with excitement, Jay stood backstage, guitar in hand, waiting for his cue to go on. His heart raced, not from nerves but from the adrenaline that always hit him before a performance. He was finally here—the big stage, the major crowd.
His career had skyrocketed in the past few months, and tonight's performance was crucial. Industry executives were out there, waiting to see if he was the real deal.
As he adjusted the strap on his guitar, Maya squeezed his arm, offering him a smile. You got this, she whispered. Jae nodded, feeling her support wrap around him like a shield.
But just as he was about to walk toward the stage, something felt off. The sound of his guitar wasn't right—a strange buzz came through the amp.
Jae's brow furrowed. He tested the strings again, only for the sound to come out completely distorted. What the ? he muttered, turning to the sound technician. The tech hurried over, checking the equipment. This was all working fine during soundcheck, Jae said, a knot forming in his stomach. The tech was flustered, plugging and unplugging wires. I don't know what happened. I swear it was perfect an hour ago.

A sinking feeling settled over Jae. He knew something was wrong. This wasn't a random malfunction. As the tech frantically worked, Jae glanced toward the back of the venue, where a familiar face caught his eye.

Trevor Jones, an up-and-coming musician who had been hovering on the edges of Jae's world for months now. Their paths had crossed more than once, and Trevor had made no secret of his jealousy. He was another artist from the streets, hungry for fame, and had been making a name for himself in the underground scene. But lately, Jae had heard whispers—rumors that Trevor was getting desperate, willing to do whatever it took to climb over Jae's rising star. Jae's eyes narrowed as he watched Trevor smirk from the shadows, arms crossed as if waiting for something to go wrong. Then, almost on cue, Jae overheard a conversation between two stagehands near the back. Did you hear what happened earlier? one of them whispered. Someone was messing with the equipment when nobody was around. Security didn't catch him, but a couple people said they saw Trevor hanging near the soundboard.

Jae's fists clenched. So that was it. Trevor had sabotaged his gear. Before he could even react, the stage manager rushed over. Jae, we've got five minutes! We need to get you out there. Is everything okay? Jae shook his head. Not yet. The sound's all wrong. Maya stepped closer, her hand on his arm. What's going on?

Jae glanced at her, then back at Trevor, who was still watching from a distance, clearly pleased with himself. Jae's pulse quickened, but he took a breath, steadying himself. He wouldn't let Trevor win, not like this. Check the cables again, Jae ordered the tech, keeping his voice calm despite the storm inside. There's something off with the setup.

The tech worked quickly, and after a tense minute, he finally fixed the issue. Got it! It's back to normal. Jae strummed his guitar, relief flooding through him as the familiar, clean sound filled the air. But the anger hadn't left. Trevor had tried to ruin his shot, and Jae wasn't going to forget it.

Let's do this, Jae said, determination hardening his voice. He glanced one more time at Trevor, locking eyes with his rival. Trevor gave him a mocking salute before disappearing into the crowd. The performance was electric. Jae poured everything he had into the music, the frustration, the betrayal—all of it bled into the chords he played and the lyrics he sang. The audience felt it, too, and by the time the set was over, the roar of applause filled the venue.

Backstage, Maya rushed to his side, her face glowing with pride. You killed it!But Jae barely smiled. His mind was still on Trevor. He knew this wouldn't be the last time Trevor would try something. Maya could see the tension in his jaw, and the tightness in his eyes. You're thinking about him, aren't you? she asked quietly, handing him a water bottle. Jae took a long drink, then wiped his face. He tried to take me down tonight. He's not gonna stop.

Maya nodded. So what do we do? We? Jae raised an eyebrow. This isn't your fight, Maya. Yes, it is, she said firmly.

We're in this together, remember? Jae sighed, but he couldn't help the gratitude that filled him when he looked at her. I'm not gonna let him win, he said, more to himself than to her. Trevor wants to play dirty, fine. But I've come too far to let anyone drag me back, Just then, his phone buzzed in his pocket. It was a message from an unknown number. Nice show tonight, Jae. Too bad about your guitar. But don't worry—next time, I'll make sure you don't get back up.

.

Jae's grip tightened around the phone, his jaw clenching. Trevor wasn't just jealous—he was dangerous. Maya leaned over, reading the message over his shoulder. He's really trying to push you, isn't he? Jae nodded, his eyes dark with resolve. Let him. He has no idea what I've survived.
And with that, Jae knew the game had changed. This wasn't just about music anymore.
This was about proving that no one—not Trevor, not his old enemies—could take away what he had built. He had fought too hard for this life, and he wasn't about to let anyone steal it from him. The battle wasn't over, but Jae was ready for whatever came next. He had Maya by his side, and he had the fire inside him that had gotten him this far. And no one—not even someone as ruthless as Trevor—could extinguish that.

9. A Father's Return

Jae had always thought he was done with family—at least, the kind you were born into. His mother's death had sealed that chapter, and his brother's betrayal had hammered the final nail in the coffin. Family, as far as Jae was concerned, was a source of pain and disappointment. So when the older man showed up after a performance one night, Jae didn't know what to make of him
It was late, the venue clearing out after another sold-out show. Jae was packing up his guitar when he noticed the man standing near the exit, watching him. The man wasn't someone he recognized, but something about his presence made Jae uneasy. His posture was relaxed but purposeful like he'd been waiting for this moment for a while. Cool performance, the man finally said, his voice gruff but steady.

Thanks, Jae responded cautiously, throwing his guitar case over his shoulder. He was about to walk past when the man took a step forward. Your mother would've been proud, you know. Jae stopped in his tracks, his chest tightening at the mention of his mother. He turned slowly, eyes narrowing. Who are you?

The man's expression softened, though there was a weight in his gaze. Name's Robert. I knew your mom... back when you were a kid. Jae tensed, his pulse quickening. He hadn't heard that name in years, not since he was a boy. His mother had mentioned Robert a few times—a friend, someone from the old neighborhood. But Jae had never thought much of it. His mother's life before him was always a mystery. Robert, Jae repeated, testing the name on his tongue. You knew my mom? What, you think that gives you the right to come find me now?

Robert didn't flinch. I'm not here for that. I'm here because I should've been a long time ago. I knew your mother... and I should've been there for you too. Jae's hands clenched into fists, his temper flaring. You don't know anything about me. Robert nodded, his eyes sad but unwavering. Maybe not. But I knew your mom well enough to know she would've wanted you to have someone, a man to look after you. I failed her in that.

Jae laughed bitterly. Look after me? Where were you when I was struggling to keep food on the table? When I was bouncing from place to place, trying to survive? You wanna play father figure now? Too late. Robert took a step closer, his voice calm but firm. I know it's too late to be a father. I'm not here to take that place.

I'm here because I see where you're headed, and I see the weight you're carrying. You've got success now, but that doesn't erase where you came from. Jae's jaw clenched as Robert's words cut through him, reopening wounds he thought he'd buried. I don't need you, Jae snapped. I made it this far without anyone. I don't need some old man showing up out of nowhere, trying to make up for lost time.

Robert didn't move, his gaze steady. I'm not trying to make up for anything. But I can see the hurt in your eyes, Jae. You've been fighting your whole life, and now that you're on top, you think you're free from all of it. But that pain... it doesn't just go away. I'm not here to save you. I'm here to tell you it's okay to face it. Jae's chest tightened, the anger mixing with something else—something deeper.
He turned away, running a hand through his hair. I've already faced it. My brother's dead, my mother's gone. That's my family. What else is there to deal with? Robert's voice softened, the edge fading. The part of you that's still carrying it all alone. You've got people around you now— Maya, your team. But you're still acting like that kid who had no one. You don't have to carry the weight of the world anymore.

Jae froze, his heart pounding. He wanted to argue, to shove Robert away and deny every word. But a part of him knew there was truth in what the man was saying. He had spent so long fighting, pushing forward, that he hadn't stopped to process the grief, the betrayal, the pain that had shaped him. What do you want from me? Jae asked quietly, still not turning to face him. Robert sighed. I don't want anything from you.

I just want you to know that you don't have to face it alone anymore. I wasn't there when you needed me, but I'm here now. And if you ever need someone to talk to, or just… someone who understands where you came from, I'm around. Jae swallowed hard, his throat tight. The idea of letting someone in, especially someone tied to his past, was terrifying. But the loneliness—the constant weight on his shoulders—was suffocating. He had Maya, but she hadn't lived his life. Robert had seen that world. He had walked those streets, too.

After a long silence, Jae finally spoke, his voice barely above a whisper. Why now? Robert hesitated before answering. Because I saw the man you're becoming, and I didn't want to miss the chance to know him.
Jae stood still for a moment, processing the words. He didn't know if he was ready to accept Robert into his life, but something about the man's sincerity softened the walls he had built around himself. Maybe it wasn't too late to deal with the parts of his past he had tried so hard to forget. Without another word, Jae nodded—just once— before walking past Robert and out into the night.

But as he stepped outside, he felt something shift inside him, a crack in the armor he had worn for so long. And for the first time in years, he wondered what it would be like to not fight every battle alone.
It was supposed to be a quiet night. Jae had just finished a long recording session and was driving home, the city lights flickering past his windows.
The streets were mostly empty, and his mind was already on the couch at home, where Maya was waiting for him. But as he turned down a familiar block, he noticed flashing blue and red lights in his rearview mirror. .

His heart sank. Jae pulled over, confused. He wasn't speeding, and his car was legit—everything was in order. Still, he felt a wave of anxiety roll through him. The cop car slowed to a stop behind him, and two officers approached his window, their expressions hard. License and registration, one of the officers said, his tone clipped. Jae handed over the documents without a word, trying to keep calm. What's this about, officer? Jae asked, forcing his voice to stay steady. The cop didn't answer. Instead, he glanced at his partner, who nodded before speaking into his radio. Jae's unease grew, his stomach knotting. Something was wrong.

We've got reports of a suspect vehicle matching this description involved in a drug deal earlier tonight, the first officer finally said. Jae's eyes widened in disbelief. What? That's a mistake. I've been at the studio all night. The officer's gaze didn't soften. Step out of the vehicle, sir. Jae froze. He knew better than to argue, especially with the way things could go south in situations like this. His fingers trembled as he unbuckled his seatbelt and stepped out of the car, his heart racing. He could already feel the tension tightening around his chest.

Before he knew it, the officer was frisking him, his hands rough and impatient. This is ridiculous, Jae muttered under his breath, but he didn't resist.
We'll see about that, the officer shot back. Turn around. Jae obeyed, his mind racing. He couldn't believe this was happening. Just when his life was starting to take off, this—this—was how things were going to go down? He had fought his whole life to get out of the streets, away from trouble.

Now, here he was, falsely accused and facing the very thing he had worked so hard to avoid. The officers were about to cuff him when a voice called out from behind. Hold up! Jae turned to see Robert striding toward them, his face set with determination. Jae hadn't even realized he had called him—his first instinct after pulling over had been to send a panicked text to Robert, and now here he was.

The officers paused, sizing up the older man. And you are? one of them asked sharply. I'm Robert Dawson, Jae's legal advisor, Robert said coolly, flashing a card from his jacket pocket. What exactly is my client being accused of? Jae's heart pounded. He hadn't expected Robert to claim he was his legal advisor, but he appreciated the quick thinking. The officers exchanged a glance, but Robert didn't give them a chance to reply before continuing. I know my rights, and I know his.

You've got nothing on him, Robert said firmly. You're accusing him of being involved in a crime? Show me the evidence. Or, better yet, explain how you've mistaken someone who's been in a studio for the last six hours for a suspect. The officers hesitated, suddenly on the defensive. The tension between them and Robert was palpable. Jae had never seen anyone stand up to the police for him like this, and it was both shocking and reassuring. One officer finally cleared his throat. We got an anonymous tip. The car matches the description. And is that enough to drag an innocent man out of his vehicle? Robert demanded. You better be sure, because if you're not, I'll make sure this department hears about it. The second officer, the one with the radio, checked something on his device. The suspect's car was a black sedan, but…His voice trailed off. This is a different model.

Robert raised an eyebrow. Exactly. You're going to arrest a man based on a vague description without even confirming the details? The first officer looked more uncertain now, glancing between Jae and Robert. We're just following procedure… And now that you've followed it,, Robert cut in, I suggest you let him go. My client has nothing to do with whatever incident you're investigating. After a tense pause, the officer sighed, stepping back. Alright. You're free to go.

Jae exhaled, the knot in his chest loosening, but his anger simmered beneath the relief. As soon as the officers left, Jae turned to Robert. Man, I don't even know what to say… Robert shook his head. You don't have to say anything. I told you, I've got your back. Jae leaned against his car, still shaken but grateful. He had always handled everything on his own—never trusting anyone to step in when things got rough.
But now, seeing Robert stand up for him, and defend him like family, something shifted. I didn't think you'd actually come, Jae admitted, rubbing the back of his neck. I'm not used to having anyone in my corner like that. Robert sighed, his face softening. I wasn't there for you when you were a kid, Jae. But I'm here now. I don't care what it takes—you're not going through this alone.

Jae looked at him, his emotions swirling. He had never asked for a father figure, but Robert's presence was forcing him to confront a part of himself he had long ignored—the part that wanted to be cared for, that needed someone to have his back. For the first time, Jae felt like he didn't have to fight every battle alone. He had someone standing with him, and as much as it scared him to trust that, it also gave him a sense of peace he hadn't known before. Thanks, Jae said quietly, his voice thick with unspoken gratitude.

Robert nodded, placing a hand on his shoulder. You're not the kid from the streets anymore. You've made something of yourself. Don't let anyone—especially the past—take that from you. Jae took a deep breath, feeling the weight of the moment. It wasn't just about getting out of this situation—it was about accepting that, maybe, just maybe, he didn't have to carry the burden of his past alone anymore. With Robert by his side, Jae realized he wasn't fighting for survival anymore. He was fighting for his future. And this time, he wasn't fighting alone.

Jae sat across from his father, Robert Dawson, at a small diner just outside the courthouse. The smell of greasy burgers and stale coffee filled the air, but Jae barely noticed. His thoughts were still tangled in the chaos of the last few hours—his arrest, the overwhelming fear of being trapped in the system, and then Robert stepping in at the last minute, pretending to be his attorney and getting him released. Now, they sat in an awkward silence, the weight of years apart hanging heavy between them. Jae glanced at Robert, taking in the man he'd only recently come to know. The older man's salt-and-pepper beard and weathered face told stories Jae had yet to hear, but his piercing eyes, so much like Jae's own, carried something that felt unfamiliar: concern.

You don't have to keep looking at me like that,mJae finally said, his voice low but steady. Robert raised an eyebrow. "Like what? Like you care. Robert leaned back in his chair, letting out a slow breath. I do care, Jae. I always have. I know it doesn't feel like it, but I'm here now. And I mean that. Jae scoffed lightly, fiddling with the handle of his coffee mug. Now? After all this time? Where were you when Mom was...when she needed help? When I needed help?

Robert flinched but didn't shy away. I was a fool, he admitted. I thought walking away was the best thing I could do back then. I didn't think I'd be any good for you or your mom. I've regretted it every damn day since. Jae's jaw tightened, his emotions swirling just beneath the surface. Regret doesn't change anything, he muttered. No, it doesn't," Robert said softly. "But actions can. And that's what I'm here to do—act. I can't change the past, but I can promise you this: I'm not going anywhere again. Whatever you need, I'll be there.

The sincerity in his voice gave Jae pause. He wanted to stay angry, to hold onto the resentment that had fueled him for so long. But part of him, the part that had always wondered what it would be like to have a father, hesitated. What made you show up today? Jae asked, his voice quieter now. Robert leaned forward, resting his forearms on the table. When I heard you were in trouble, I couldn't ignore it. I've been keeping tabs on you, Jae. Watching from the sidelines. I didn't know if you'd want me around, but when I saw my son needed me…He trailed off, shaking his head. "I wasn't about to let you face this alone.

Jae studied him for a long moment, the tension in his shoulders softening slightly. "I've been doing things alone for a long time," he admitted. "It's hard to imagine it any other way. You don't have to anymore, Robert said firmly. Let me prove it to you. The conversation shifted after that, turning lighter as Robert asked about Jae's music. They spent hours talking—about the songs Jae had written, the struggles he'd faced, and the dreams he still clung to. Robert shared bits of his own life, stories that gave Jae a glimpse into the man he was trying to become.

By the time they left the diner, the distance between them felt a little smaller. As they stood by Jae's car, Robert placed a hand on his shoulder. I'm proud of you, son, he said. "For everything you've done and everything you're going to do. And I'll be here, no matter what. Jae nodded, a small flicker of hope sparking in his chest. We'll see, he said, but his tone lacked the sharpness it had before. As he watched Robert walk away, Jae realized that, for the first time, he wasn't just strumming through the pain. Maybe, just maybe, he was starting to play a melody of healing.

11. The World Tour

Some weeks later Jae sat at the kitchen table, staring at the email on his phone. His heart was pounding, and his mind was racing faster than he could keep up with. This was it— the opportunity he'd been grinding for, praying for, every sleepless night and every aching finger on his guitar leading up to this moment. A world tour. Not just any tour, but a headlining gig across Europe, Asia, and South America. Months of sold-out arenas, performing in cities he'd only ever dreamed of. His music had officially gone global, and now it was time to claim his place. But there was a catch.

The tour would last nearly a year. He'd be on the road, gone for months at a time, with barely any breaks in between. It was everything he had worked for—but as Jae read the details over again, he couldn't help but feel a tight knot form in his stomach. Maya. The thought of leaving her behind, of missing so much time together, tore at him. They had built a life together, navigating the ups and downs as a team, leaning on each other through every challenge. And now, he was faced with a choice that could rip that apart.

The sound of Maya's footsteps approached. She walked into the room, her eyes lighting up when she saw Jae. Hey, you've been quiet. Everything okay?" she asked, leaning over the table to kiss him on the cheek. Jae blinked, snapping out of his thoughts. He forced a smile, but it didn't quite reach his eyes. Yeah... yeah, everything's fine.

Maya frowned, noticing the tension in his expression. What is it? she pressed, sitting across from him. Jae took a deep breath, sliding his phone across the table so she could see the email. I got it, he said softly. The tour. It's huge. World tour, headline act. Maya's eyes widened as she read the email, her face breaking into a smile. Oh my god, Jae! That's incredible! This is everything you've been working for.

Jae nodded, but the weight on his chest didn't ease. Yeah, it is... but it's months, Maya. I'd be gone for almost a year. I don't even know how we'd... I don't want to leave you for that long. The excitement in Maya's eyes faded, replaced by understanding and concern. She set the phone down, her fingers nervously playing with the edge of her sleeve. That's a long time, she admitted softly, her gaze dropping to the table.

Silence hung between them, heavy and thick. Jae's heart ached as he watched her struggle with the news. He could see the conflict in her eyes—she wanted to be happy for him, but the reality of their situation was sinking in fast. I don't know what to do, Jae finally said, his voice breaking the silence. This tour... it could change everything. But I don't want to lose us in the process.

Maya looked up at him, her eyes filled with love and pain. Jae, this is your dream. I knew who you were when I fell in love with you—a musician, someone with a fire that couldn't be put out. I never wanted to hold you back from that. But you're not holding me back, Jae protested. I don't want to go if it means losing what we have. Maya took his hand, squeezing it gently. I don't want you to feel like you have to choose between me and your dream. You've worked so hard for this, and I'm proud of you. I don't want to be the reason you don't take this chance. Jae felt his chest tighten. He knew Maya was trying to be supportive, but he could hear the uncertainty in her voice. She was scared, just like he was.

What if I take the tour, and things change between us? Jae asked quietly. What if we drift apart? Maya's eyes glistened with unshed tears. What if we don't? she whispered. What if we're strong enough to get through it? We've made it through so much already, Jae. This will be hard, I know that. But I also know we can survive it, if we both want to. Jae's mind raced. The idea of being apart from Maya for months on end terrified him. But this opportunity... it was everything he had worked for, everything he had sacrificed for. Could he really turn it down? Maya wiped away a stray tear and gave him a small, sad smile. I love you, Jae. And no matter what happens, I'll always support you. But you need to make this decision for you. I don't want you to regret anything.Jae looked down at their joined hands, feeling the weight of the decision pressing down on him. He loved Maya more than anything, but his music was a part of his soul, the one thing that had kept him alive all these years. Could he have both? Could they survive the distance, the time apart? He swallowed hard, meeting Maya's eyes. I don't want to lose you.

Maya shook her head, her smile bittersweet. "You won't. We'll figure it out. I promise. The words hung in the air, a fragile promise between them, full of love and fear. Jae knew this decision would change everything, no matter what he chose. And as he held Maya's hand, he realized that sometimes, even with love, there were no easy answers.

Jae sat in silence for what felt like an eternity, his thoughts a chaotic storm inside his head. The weight of the decision pressed heavily on his chest, the tour, his dream, Maya—all swirling together in a way that felt impossible to untangle. He looked at her, sitting across from him, her eyes full of love, understanding, and fear. She had always been there, a constant source of support in his life, but he knew the toll this would take on both of them.

Finally, Jae took a deep breath and squeezed Maya's hand, his voice low and steady. I'm going to take the tour. Maya's eyes flickered with surprise, and though he could see the pain behind her gaze, she nodded slowly. Okay, she whispered, her voice soft but strong But, Jae continued, his grip on her hand tightening, we're going to figure this out. I don't want to lose us, Maya. I can't. We'll make it work. I'll come back whenever I can. We'll talk every day, FaceTime, whatever it takes. You'll visit me whenever it's possible. We won't let this pull us apart.

Maya's tears finally spilled over, but she smiled through them. We'll make it work, she echoed, her voice shaking but filled with determination. "I believe in us, Jae. He leaned over, pulling her into his arms. The warmth of her body against his was a comfort, a promise that even though things were about to change, they would fight for what they had.

We're not like everyone else, Jae murmured into her hair. We've been through too much. This is just one more thing, and we'll get through it. Maya nodded against his chest, holding onto him tightly. I'm scared, but I trust you. I trust us. Jae kissed the top of her head, feeling both the weight of the decision and the relief of having made it. He wasn't naïve—he knew it would be hard.

There would be moments of doubt, loneliness, and fear. But the love they had was real, and he was determined not to let distance or time change that. Over the following weeks, they made plans, mapped out how they would stay connected while Jae was on the road. Maya even started working on a new series of paintings, inspired by the idea of distance and love. They spoke about her joining him on tour for a few stops, and though the thought of being apart for so long was daunting, they found strength in knowing they were facing it together. The night before Jae was set to leave, they sat together in their small apartment, wrapped in each other's arms, the quiet hum of the city outside. No matter what happens out there, I'll always come back to you, Jae said, his voice a soft promise. Maya smiled, her eyes shining. And I'll be right here, waiting.

13. Through The Light

As the tour bus pulled away the next day, Jae glanced back at Maya standing on the curb, waving him off with a brave smile on her face. His heart ached, but it also swelled with love. He knew this journey would be long and challenging, but as the city faded behind him, Jae held onto one truth— he wasn't just chasing his dream; he was building a future with the woman who had his heart.

And no matter where the road took him, he knew he'd always find his way back to her. As the months passed, Jae's tour became a whirlwind of success. Sold-out arenas, glowing reviews, and the rush of performing to thousands of people each night filled him with a sense of accomplishment he had only dreamed of. But every time the lights dimmed and the crowds dispersed, there was an emptiness that tugged at him. He missed Maya—her laugh, her touch, the simple comfort of being with her. They had stuck to their plan: phone calls late at night, video chats when time zones allowed, and short visits whenever Maya could break away from her own work. It was hard, harder than either of them had anticipated, but they held on, fighting to keep the connection alive. Through the highs and lows, they never let go of each other, even when distance seemed determined to push them apart. One night, after a particularly grueling performance in Tokyo, Jae sat in his hotel room, his guitar resting in his lap.

The city buzzed outside his window, but all he could think about was home. Maya. She had become his anchor, the reason he kept pushing forward, and the thought of losing her weighed heavily on his mind. As he strummed a quiet melody, his phone buzzed beside him. It was a text from Maya: I miss you so much. Can't wait to see you again soon. Love you always. Jae smiled, the ache in his chest easing slightly. He texted her back: Not much longer. I'm coming home soon. We'll be together again, and this time, I'm not going anywhere.He stared at the screen for a moment before setting the phone down. The tour had given him everything he'd worked for—fame, recognition, and success. But it had also shown him that none of it mattered without Maya by his side. The music, the crowds, the applause—they were fleeting. What he had with her was real.

As the final leg of the tour approached, Jae made a decision. Once it was over, he was done chasing. He would come back to Maya, and they would build the life they had always dreamed of—together. But as Jae packed up his guitar and prepared for his final show, he couldn't shake the feeling that life had more twists in store for them. He had conquered so much, fought through the darkness of his past, and found love and success in ways he never imagined. But the road ahead was still uncertain, full of challenges he couldn't yet see.

The night of the final show came, and as Jae stood backstage, ready to step out onto the biggest stage of his career, he knew this wasn't the end of his story. It was just another chapter. As the lights came up and the crowd roared his name, Jae took a deep breath, his fingers brushing the strings of his guitar. He smiled, thinking of Maya, waiting for him on the other side of this last performance. Whatever came next, they would face it together. And so, as the music swelled and the stage lights bathed him in their glow, Jay stepped forward, ready for whatever the future had in store. In the quiet after the storm, Jae looked back at the path he had walked, knowing the shadows would always be a part of him.

The roar of the crowd was a distant memory now. Jae sat quietly in the back of the car as it weaved through the familiar streets of the city he called home. The last six months had been a whirlwind—stadiums packed with fans singing his songs, interviews with people who wanted to dissect his soul, and long, lonely nights in hotel rooms staring at the ceiling, wondering if Maya was doing the same.

The tour had been everything he'd dreamed of as a kid strumming his guitar in the alleyways, but it had also been a stark reminder of what dreams could cost. He rubbed his hands together, staring at the wedding band on his finger. It had been a lifeline, a small tether to the love that had kept him grounded.

The car pulled into the driveway, and Jae stepped out, his heart pounding in a way it never had on stage. The house was just as he'd left it—Maya's touch visible in the neat flowerbeds and the wind chimes dancing softly in the breeze. He hesitated for a moment before heading to the door, his guitar case slung over his shoulder.

When he walked inside, the smell of something warm and familiar greeted him. Maya appeared in the doorway of the kitchen, her face lighting up when she saw him. She didn't run to him or make a grand gesture; she just smiled, a simple, quiet smile that said, I've been waiting for you. Hey, she said softly. Hey," Jae replied, his voice catching in his throat. He dropped his bag and crossed the room to her, wrapping his arms around her waist. For a moment, they just stood there, holding onto each other as if the months apart had never happened.

How was the tour? she asked, leaning back to look at him. Unreal, he admitted. But lonely. I missed you. I missed you too, she said, brushing a hand against his cheek. But I'm proud of you, Jae. You did it. They moved to the couch, and Jae recounted stories from the road—the highs, the lows, and everything in between. Maya listened intently, laughing at his anecdotes and squeezing his hand during the tougher moments.

But as the conversation wound down, Jae's tone grew serious. "You know, Maya, for a long time I thought success was the endgame. I thought if I could just get there, everything would make sense. But out there on that stage, with all those people cheering… I realized it doesn't mean much if I don't have you to share it with.

Maya smiled, her eyes glistening. You've always had me, Jae. You just needed to believe it. He nodded, taking her hand in his. I do. And I've learned something else too. Life isn't about reaching some perfect place where everything is okay. It's about the journey—strumming through the pain, singing through the joy, and finding meaning in the mess. Maya rested her head on his shoulder, her fingers intertwining with his. So, what's next for you, Mr. Rockstar?

Jae grinned, a mischievous glint in his eye. I was thinking… maybe a quieter gig for a while. Something closer to home. As they sat there, the clock ticking softly in the background, the world seemed to fade away, leaving just the two of them in their bubble of love and understanding. But Jae knew the story wasn't over. His phone buzzed on the coffee table, an unknown number lighting up the screen.

He glanced at it, his brow furrowing slightly. Maya noticed and looked up at him. Are you going to get that?" she asked. Jae hesitated, then shook his head, pulling her closer. Not tonight. Outside, the wind chimes sang their quiet melody, and somewhere in the distance, the world waited.

To be continued...

Acknowledgements

Writing, In The Shadows of Jae, has been a journey of reflection, growth, and discovery, and I couldn't have done it alone.

First, I want to thank my family and friends, whose unwavering support and encouragement kept me going, even when the road seemed uncertain. To my readers, your belief in this story has been a light through the darkness—thank you for giving it a place in your heart.

A special thank you to everyone who inspired the characters and moments in this book. Your stories, resilience, and strength have shaped more than just words on a page; they've given life to the soul of this story.

And lastly, to all those who strive through their own darkness, know that dawn always follows. This book is for you.

With gratitude,
Jae Lavell